I0742088
FOOP
THUNK

CLOP
CLOP
SHIT!!
SHUT UP.
chk
WHAT... WAS THAT?!
WHAT WAS WHAT?
HA
HA
HA
HA
YOU MISSED A TARGET 20 PACES AWAY. IS YOUR EYESIGHT FAILING ALREADY?
I'D BE THE FIRST TO ADMIT IT IF I COULDN'T SEE IN THE DARK ANYMORE!
MAYBE WE SHOULD LET THE YOUNG MEN HUNT FOR US FROM NOW ON.
ARNE.
YOU'RE RIGHT. I'M SORRY.

I WONDER WHAT WILL BECOME OF THAT BUCK.
WELL, AFTER SUCH A NARROW ESCAPE AND HOW LOUD YOU YELLED, I'M SURE EVERY DEER WILL AVOID THE AREA FOR A WEEK!
NO, I MEANT... HOW OLD DO YOU THINK HE WAS?
MATURE, I'D SAY?
PERHAPS HE'LL NEVER DIE AN HONORABLE DEATH. PERHAPS ONE DAY HE'LL JUST... FALL DOWN AND NEVER GET UP.
RUNE, I'M SORRY ABOUT THE 'OLD MAN' JOKES. I DIDN'T MEAN TO HURT YOU.
NO, YOU'RE RIGHT. MAYBE WE WERE TOO GOOD AT THE JOB OF WARRIOR. BUT NOW... WELL, NOW WHAT?
WHAT DO YOU MEAN?
WHEN YOU AND I CAN NO LONGER SEE WELL ENOUGH TO SHOOT STRAIGHT... WHAT ARE WE? WHAT HAVE WE ACCOMPLISHED? WHAT DO WE DO THEN?

I DIDN'T EXPECT TO BE PRODDED ON THE MEANING OF LIFE THIS EVENING. IT'S JUST A STRAY SHOT. FORGET I SAID ANYTHING. PLEASE.
YOU'RE RIGHT. I'LL SEE YOU TOMORROW.
shnk

LATER...

CH- KOOM

RUMBLE
RUMBLE

BOOM!

WHAT THE-?!

DID A TREE FALL?!
I HOPE IT DIDN'T HIT ARNE'S..

SHWING

RUMBLE
OH. UH.

HELLO.
HELLO.
I'M SORRY, DID YOU LOSE YOUR WAY IN THE STORM?
HEH. I MIGHT HAVE.
WELL, IF YOU'D LIKE YOU CAN COME IN.
ARE YOU SURE?

I DON'T HAVE MUCH, BUT I SUPPOSE A FIRE AND A ROOF IS BETTER THAN RAIN AND WET FUR!
shk
PLEASE, HAVE A SEAT BY THE FIRE.

I NOTICED YOU DIDN'T MENTION THE THUNDER AS ONE OF THE UNPLEASANTRIES OUTSIDE.

WELL, I'VE ALWAYS LIKED THE SOUND OF THUNDER.

I'VE PRAYED TO THOR EVER SINCE I WAS A BOY. IT REMINDS ME OF HIM, EVEN IN... DARKER MOMENTS.
DARKER?
CLUNK
IT'S NOTHING. SO, WHERE DO YOU COME FROM?

OH, MANY PLACES.
SOME YOU'VE BEEN TO, SOME I'M SURE YOU'VE ONLY HEARD OF.

I'D LOVE TO HEAR OF THEM, THEN!
I MEAN, IF YOU WERE PLANNING TO KILL ME YOU WOULD'VE DONE IT WHEN I OPENED THE DOOR!
TRUE, BUT THEN YOUR PRAYER WOULD'VE BEEN ANSWERED, YES?

MY... WHAT??

YOUR PRAYER. YOU FEAR NEVER JOINING YOUR FOREFATHERS IN VALHALLA, YES?
I MADE NO SUCH PRAYER! WERE YOU FOLLOWING US?
I'VE KNOWN YOU LONG ENOUGH - I HEAR YOU EVEN WHEN YOU DON'T SPEAK, RUNE.
SNK
HOW DO YOU KNOW MY-
CRACKLE
CHA-KOOM
...THOR.

ZZT
CLUNK
WHY ARE YOU HERE?
I CAME TO SEE MY OLD FRIEND!
IT'S HOW YOU SPEAK OF YOURSELF.
I WON'T PRETEND I DIDN'T NOTICE HOW YOU SAID THAT.
...
WAS I RIGHT?
AM I OLD?
ABOUT WHAT?
I...DON'T THINK THAT WAS THE ACTUAL QUESTION, WAS IT?

WILL MY LIFE HAVE ANY MEANING AFTER I'M GONE?

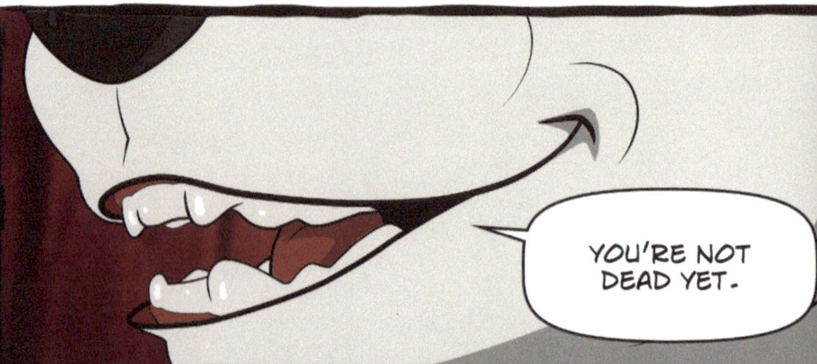

YOU'RE NOT DEAD YET.

WHY HAVE YOU NEVER MARRIED?

I...

NEVER EVEN DROPPED YOUR TROUSERS WITH ANOTHER.

IT'S MY GREATEST SECRET.

SAY IT ANYWAY.

I LIKE MEN.

MAYBE... ONE IN PARTICULAR?
BUT I WOULD NEVER... FOR A MAN TO TAKE ANOTHER LIKE THAT IS SO VIOLENT TO HIS HONOR.
...ARNE.
I COULD NEVER DO THAT TO ARNE. HE IS... GENTLE WITH ME.
HAT'S ALL THAT ELD YOU BACK??
FUCKING MIDGARDIANS.
RUNE, I THINK I HAVE ONE MORE LESSON TO TEACH YOU TONIGHT.
WAIT - WHAT?
THAT EVERYTHING YOU JUST SAID IS BULLSHIT.

YOU... WHAT?
DON'T TELL ME YOU'RE SO REPRESSED THAT YOUR MANHOOD ISN'T LENGTHENING RIGHT NOW.
I... MAYBE.
GOOD. NOW IT'S GETTING AWKWARD STANDING HERE NAKED.
JOIN ME.
NO! SAY IT!
...YES.
BUT... WHAT ARE WE GOING TO DO?

WE'RE GOING TO FUCK, AND MAYBE BY THE END YOU'LL REALIZE WHAT THE GODS ACTUALLY THINK.
YOU'RE GOING TO—
NO.
YOU ARE.
NOW UNDRESS AND STICK THAT WOOD IN ME. YOU'VE ONLY GOT TONIGHT.
YOU MEAN... THE GODS DO IT...?
IT FEELS GOOD BOTH WAYS. NOW HOP ON!

Shff
HNNG!
ARE YOU ALL RIGHT?
YES. YOU FEEL GOOD. KEEP GOING.
nudge
OH YES...

WOW.
heh
hump
hump
hump
IT REALLY—
YOU LIKE HOW
I FEEL?
YOU FEEL
GREAT.
YOU CAN GO
FASTER,
YOU KNOW.
JUST *GRUNT*
DIDN'T WANT TO
HURT YOU.
FP
FLP
HUMP
FFP
SLK
SLK
FFP

hah
hah
SHHLP
THERE
YOU GO.
heh
PLAP
SLAP
FFP
CLAP
SHLP
FFP
PLAP
SCHLP
FLFP
thnrob
plap
clap plap
ffp
OOH.. I'M
FEELING...
THAT KNOT

NNG!
hahh
shlp
hah
hah
YOU WERE...
NOT WHAT I
EXPECTED!
I THOUGHT ONCE
YOU FINALLY FELT
THE INSIDE OF A
MAN YOU'D BEAT
MY ASS TO DEATH.
YOU'RE A RARE FIND!

YOU... YOU HAVEN'T COME YET.

PLEASE, LET ME...

NO, SAVE THAT FOR YOUR LOVE! DON'T LET ME BE YOUR FIRST FOR EVERYTHING!

BUT I WANT TO PLEASE YOU, TOO!

I'VE NEVER FELT THIS WAY — I NEVER WOULD HAVE! PLEASE?

CHUCKLE
ARNE WOULD BE A FOOL NOT TO ACCEPT YOU AS HIS LOVER.
GO AHEAD. WITH YOUR MOUTH.
HOMM

slrp
NNG!
HAH!
HUFF
ARE YOU CONVINCED? OR DO YOU STILL THINK THIS IS DISHONOR?
HEH. ALL FORGOTTEN.
CHUCKLE THEN MY WORK HERE IS DONE.

WELL THEN. GOODBYE, RUNE.

I HOPE YOU REMEMBER WHAT YOU LEARNED TONIGHT!

WAIT!

WILL YOU... WILL YOU COME BACK?
I WANT TO SEE YOU AGAIN. LIKE THIS.

OF ALL THINGS, I HOPE I'M NOT LOOKING AT A COWARD.
WHAT?!

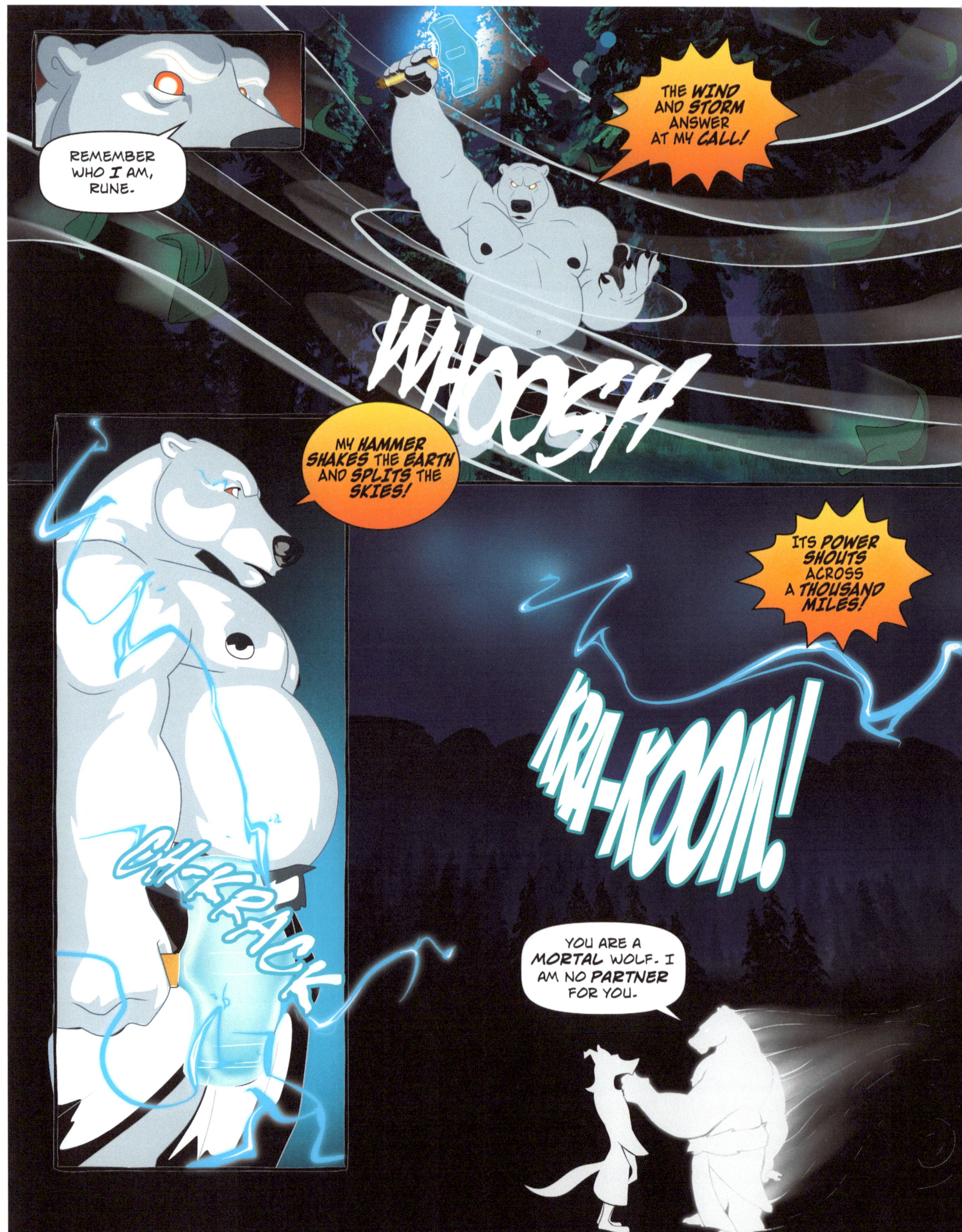

REMEMBER WHO I AM, RUNE.
THE WIND AND STORM ANSWER AT MY CALL!
MY HAMMER SHAKES THE EARTH AND SPLITS THE SKIES!
WHOOSH
ITS POWER SHOUTS ACROSS A THOUSAND MILES!
CH-KRACK
KRA-KOOM!
YOU ARE A MORTAL WOLF. I AM NO PARTNER FOR YOU.

GO TO YOUR LOVE. YOUR REAL LOVE.
BE BRAVE ENOUGH TO LAY YOURSELF BARE IN MORE THAN BATTLE. TO SPEAK THE WORDS OF YOUR HEART.
THEN HE WILL NOT BE AFRAID.
DO THIS, AND I WILL SEND A SIGN THAT YOUR LOVE HOLDS MY FAVOR.
GO NOW, WARRIOR!
LET NOT THE TIME FLY FURTHER!
SHOOM

DNK
DNK
ARNE.
IT'S ME.

RUNE! WHAT
ON EARTH?
ARNE. PLEASE.
LET ME COME IN?

IT'S THE MIDDLE
OF THE NIGHT!
PLEASE? IT'S
IMPORTANT.

OKAY, GET IN
OUT OF THE
RAIN.
I, UM...
HAVE TO TELL
YOU SOMETHING.
WHAT'S
HAPPENED?

I... I LOVE YOU.
I LOVE YOU TOO, YOU KNOW THAT! NOW, WHAT IS IT?
THAT WAS IT. I LOVE YOU.
...
I DON'T UNDERSTAND.
NOT LIKE FRIENDS, OR BROTHERS, THOUGH YOU HAVE BEEN BOTH TO ME.
BUT THE OTHER KIND.
THE STRONGER KIND.

BUT...I'M A MALE.

YOU SHOULD LOVE SOMEONE WHO IS A FIT FOR YOU AND YOUR... WELL, ANY MAN'S NEEDS.

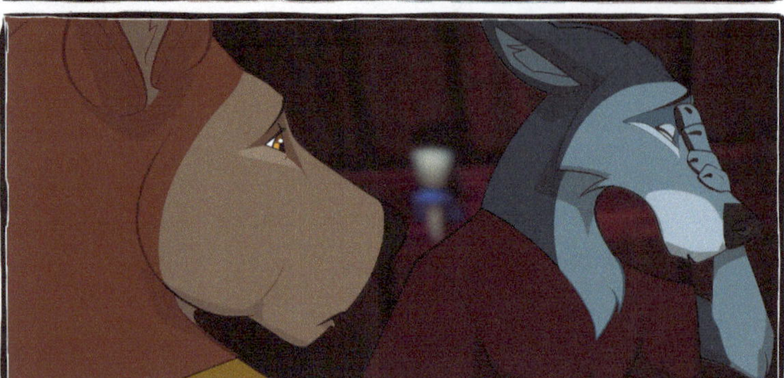

ARNE, IF YOU WOULD HAVE ME I WOULD FULFILL ALL YOUR NEEDS AND MORE.
YOU MEAN YOU WOULD—
BUT NO!
I WOULD NEVER DO THAT TO YOU. YOU'VE BEEN MY FRIEND SINCE WE WERE PUPS!
I KNOW— I KNOW YOU'D NEVER HURT ME. THAT'S WHY—
NO, STOP.

I WON'T SAY THAT I HAVEN'T FELT... THINGS FOR YOU.
MANY TIMES I'VE HAD TO HIDE MYSELF.
I DIDN'T KNOW THAT. BUT... SO HAVE I, WITH YOU.

BUT WE... COULD NOT RISK ANGERING THE GODS—
THAT'S ANOTHER THING I CAME TO TELL YOU! THOR CAME TO ME TONIGHT!
HE PROMISED TO SHOW YOU A SIGN THAT HE SHOWS YOU AND I FAVOR. THAT WE CAN BE TOGETHER!
WHAT?!
YES! AND HE TOLD ME — THAT THE GODS DO NOT FROWN ON THIS. WE MORTALS MADE THAT UP!
I LOVE YOU, ARNE I NEED YOU WITH ME.
BOOM

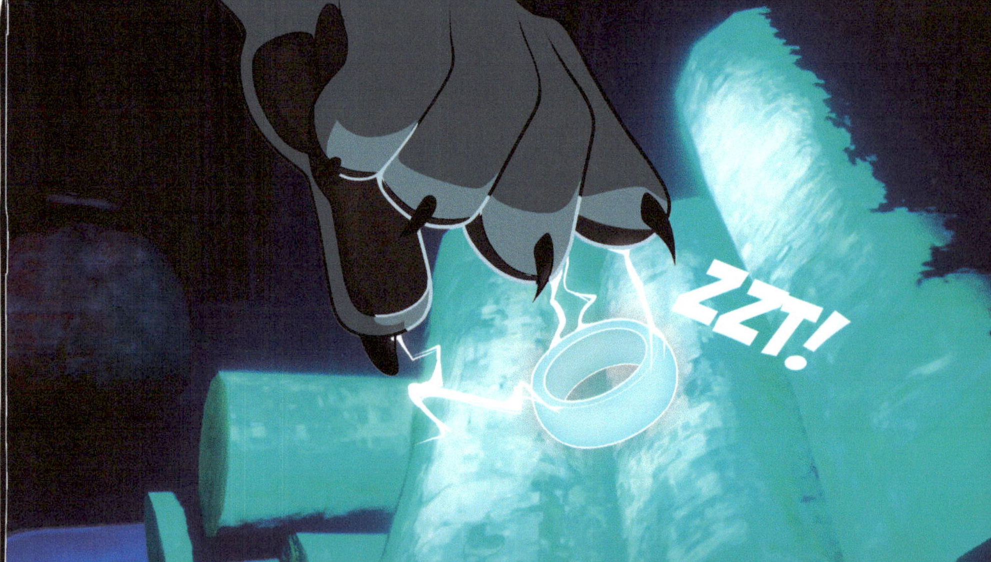

ZZT!

THAT'S... IT IS!
FORGED BY MJOLLNIR ITSELF.

I, UM---I NEED TIME.

OLD FRIEND. WILL YOU GIVE ME TIME?

---YES. OF COURSE.

HEH.

rub

NOW, GO GET SOME SLEEP.
OKAY.
KEEP THAT, UNTIL THEN
ALL RIGHT.
nod
THE NEXT MORNING...

ARNE!
HI!
UHH...
MAY I
COME IN?
I UM...
I DIDN'T
SLEEP MUCH.
ME
EITHER.
I DON'T KNOW
HOW THIS WILL
WORK. ANY OF IT.
BUT...
YES. I WILL
TRY, WITH YOU.
dnk
dnk dnk

SHOOM

I DIDN'T EXPECT IT TO FEEL LIKE THAT!
LET'S GO AGAIN.
MY... MY TROUSERS ARE GETTING A LITTLE TIGHT.
I'M THE SAME.

shff
wag
wag
wag

I LIKE THIS.
HRRM.
BUT WHAT ELSE?
THOR GAVE ME SOME IDEAS.
HM?
OH WOW.
lick
homm

heh
hah
hoh
slk
slk
hmm
:squeeze:
Ooh fuck
slk
slk
NNG!

nng!
SK
hom
SK SK
SK
mmf
I'M GETTING CLOSE!
pah!
NOT YET!
HUFF CAN I...
CAN I TRY YOURS?

CHUCKLE
OF COURSE!
C'MERE!
IT'S ALL YOURS.

lick
homm
HEH. THIS FEELS
GRUNT
REALLY GOOD ON THE
RECEIVING END!
sjk
slp
sjk
sjk
hmmg

HAH. CLOSE.
I DON'T KNOW ABOUT YOU YET, BUT AT MY AGE I ONLY HAVE ONE SHOT IN ME AND THEN I NEED A LONG REST.
HONESTLY, I'M THE SAME.
...
YOU GO FIRST.
WHO'S FIRST?
AT WHAT? HAHAHA.

... MY MANHOOD JUST THROBBED.
SO I JUST...?
I'M READY.
hah!
hrk!
ffp

OH MY THAT'S... WOW.
IT'S THAT GOOD?
MMF! I MAY HAVE OFFERED MY RUMP TOO SOON!
WHY?
I THINK YOU'RE GOING TO MAKE ME CUM!
THEN I KNOW WHAT TO DO NEXT.
PLAP
PLAP
PLAP
PLAP
PLAP
PLAP
Hah
hah
PLAP
PLAP
PLAP
PLAP
PLAP
PLAP
fp plap
fp
shp
hahh
plap
ffp
plap

FFP
PLP
SLP
SHP
CLP
PLAP
OH!
ARE YOU ALL RIGHT?
ANY MORE, AND I'LL—
NNG!
shlp

MY TURN.
SHOW ME.
I WON'T LAST LONG!
I DON'T THINK I WILL, EITHER.

AH HAH
LAP
PLAP
FFP
FFP FAP
FFP
FFP
HUFF ARE YOU SURE?
I—
I NEED TO—
PLAP
PLAP
PLAP
PLAP
PLAP
PLAP
FFP
SPLOOT
AH!

SHP
PLAP
FLP
NNG!
FFP
SHP
PLP
THP
SHP
PLP
PLP
THP
SHP
PLAP
SHP
FUCK I CAN
FEEL YOUR
KNOT.
I'M KEEPING
IT OUT.
PLAP FLP THP
PLP
FFP
PLAP
FFP
THP
FFP
PLAP
NO. IN.
DO IT NOW.

SQUEEZE
NNG!
POP!
OH SHIT...
SQUIRT

FFP
FFP
PLAP
FFP
THP
FFP
PLAP
PLAP
THP
SHP
PLAP
SHP
PLAP
AH!
OHH!
HAHHHHN NNGGG...

HAH
HUFF
HUFF
HAGH. SO...
WE'RE STUCK...
FOR A WHILE.
HEH
...
MY FEET ARE
FALLING ASLEEP.
HA
HA
HA
HA
HA!
LET'S GET MORE
COMFORTABLE.
LET ME—

OOHOOH!
THAT TICKLES
IN THERE!

SO... DID THOR
FUCK YOU
LIKE THIS?

WHAT? NO. WAIT,
HOW DID YOU KNOW
HE AND I—?

WELL LAST NIGHT I
REALIZED... IT WOULD
HAVE TAKEN MORE THAN
JUST A TALK TO GIVE YOU
THE COURAGE TO TELL
ME WHAT YOU DID.

UM... YES. BUT HE DIDN'T FUCK ME. I FUCKED HIM!
REALLY!
HE SAID...
HE SAID HE THOUGHT YOU SHOULD BE MY FIRST. TO BE UNDER MY TAIL, I MEAN.
HMM...

I THINK... MAYBE WE WAITED TOO LONG, ARNE.
WE SHOULD'VE DONE THIS WHEN WE WERE YOUNG.
I'M SORRY I NEVER SPOKE UP.
ME, TOO. BUT YOU AND I STILL HAVE PLENTY OF TIME LEFT. I'M GLAD WE FIGURED IT OUT AT LAST!
AND AFTER YOUR COCK SOFTENS, I THINK MINE NEEDS TO TRY OUT YOUR ASS AGAIN!
HAHAHAHA!
END